Amazing Adventures of Minecraft Steve Book 1

Wimpy Fan

ISBN: 978-1518765858

Dedicated to Holly & Olivia.

CONTENTS

ACKNOWLEDGMENTS

This is an unofficial Minecraft short story which has been produced as a piece of fan fiction. Minecraft is a registered trademark of Mojang AB, and respective owners who hasn't authorized, sponsored or endorsed this book.

CHAPTER 1

Beyond the sonorous thumping of the blood in his ears, there was the calming, rhythmic lulling of water dripping into a still pool. It was soothing, there in the darkness, to hear a familiar tone, reminiscent of the laborious swings of his pickaxe—which he fumbled around to feel for. Despite the hard, cold rock at his finger tips, there was a warm and soft plushness that cushioned what should have been a devastating fall. Peeking one eye up, he could faintly see the distant twinkle of daylight that had abandoned him deep into the mine shaft. He should have known better not to dig himself into these situations, but he was still but a novice miner.

A sigh accompanied the sound of his fingers gently prodding towards his stone pickaxe, which was just barely out of his reach, and he hoped it had been his own relief that had caused the noise. As he retrieved the tool, he was curious once more about the furry mass that he had been laying upon, and carefully maneuvered his way back a few paces. Even with the light of the pixelated sun so far above him, he hardly had to guess what creature bore him upon its back.

"Gah!" he cried out as he failed his pickaxe towards what lay beneath him, as if he was not certain it was already resting.

Jumping off of his luxurious makeshift bed, he realized that it was the remains of some giant cave spider, which had broken his fall. At least, that's how he hoped it had been slain, or else there might have been much more dangerous things down there than a mere spider. Swinging the pickaxe over his shoulder, he looked down at the fallen foe and tried to remain calm.

"It's just a spider, Steve, you've seen them

before," he tried to console himself, but his voice was trembling fiercely. Trying on a more masculine and confident tone, he went on, "you've fought them before, you've won before. It's just a spider—like a wolf, but with eight legs. No, don't imagine that!"

He shivered and shook the terrifying thought out of his head, instead adjusting his sweaty grip on the stone pickaxe he clutched far too tightly. It hardly mattered what the creature was that laid before him, as it was already dead.

Before thinking to scavenge the remains for something useful, Steve looked back up towards the slim shaft he had clumsily fallen through. It was far too steep to climb back up, and grew narrower the nearer it got to the surface, so mining his way back up seemed improbable. But he knew that there were tunnels all over this rigid mountain, with entrances hiding everywhere. There must have been another way out, there just must have been.

Steve was certain that the first thing he had to do was to recover his bearings, and the easiest way to do that was to first illuminate his surroundings. Sifting through his inventory, his nervous hands came across his set of crafted torches, which were bunched in one corner beneath his water bucket and some spare materials. He plucked just one and raised it, striking it lit before being stunned completely stiff.

The chamber was massive: a vast, desolate cavern with what seemed like a endless labyrinth of shafts and tunnels—none of which seemed very inviting. Though is was a daunting challenge, he was surely glad that he was entirely alone. Swallowing the anxious lump in his throat, Steve carefully sneaked over to the hanging wall nearest to the middle of the cave and planted the torch along the flat side of some indeterminate rock.

"Okay, now which way to the village?" he murmured to himself thoughtfully, trying to remember which direction he had been facing when he had plummeted head first into the darkness, as if

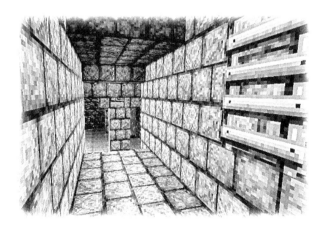

someone could ever remember that. "I was on the

West side of the mountain, with the sun going down in that direction, the light should fall through the shaft to the East."

He tried to get a better look at the angle at which the light from the sun broke in, but it was a difficult thing to do. As he squinted up at the break in the rock, he could see the way it gradually turned to soil, and then spotted the trim of some foliage. With a definite nod, he chose the most likely direction, though it still seemed entirely random, and set off in it. Taking another torch, Steve jumped over a few short blocks before placing a marker above the tunnel of his choice.

As he stepped through the narrow passage, Steve found a sharp turn and followed it dutifully. However, upon taking it, he found himself face to flat face with nothing but a dead end. Growling and glowering at the obstruction, he hit a few blocks with his pickaxe, only to come up with nothing but some building materials and a slightly more worn axe. It was just his luck, or lack there of.

Steve returned to the main cave and curmudgeonly plucked the torch from its place above the useless shaft, instead placing it above the tunnel just to the left. Using his worthless collection of rock pixels, he built up a wall over the previous passage as to deter him from trying it again. He would never find the veins of tin and gold that awaited him a few blocks further down that shaft, but he pressed on diligently.

The next tunnel did seem a good deal deeper, as he could peer only so far into the shadows before his vision was lost in the suffocating darkness. This was not uncommon though, as the light levels fell so far when one mined beyond the reaches of the sun. The first few blocks were void of any trial or trouble, and as much as he craved the adventure of scaling mountainsides and delving into deep and deserted mine shafts, he didn't mind a spell of smooth sailing either.

CHAPTER 2

The elastic pull of a bow string caught Steve's attention, and he hurriedly dodged to the nearest wall to take cover. He was alarmed, though, by the threatening arrow that stuck straight out of the wall directly beside him. Quickly digging through his inventory, Steve managed to retrieve a bow of his own crafting, though he only ever had the chance to

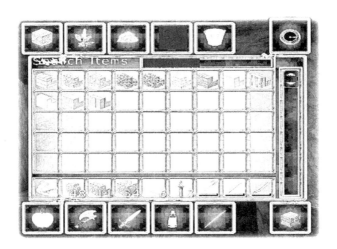

use it when hunting rather than for survival.

Steve hurdled over a steep drop and landed in the recessed space of a few blocks that shielded him from the next barrage of arrows—of which there were three. He clumsily raised his own bow and looked out into the poorly lit chamber. The shifting and clacking of bones alerted him to his enemies: a group of hostile skeletons. Their undead bodies wreaked of dust and decay, and their arrows flew truer than any weakened man's muscles could merit. And Steve, ill-prepared for the encounter, knew that fighting them off could be a much greater feat than he could accomplish alone.

Following the inaccurate shots of his own, Steve already knew that he hadn't brought along enough arrows to fend them off, nor was he proficient enough to gamble to time picking them off while simultaneously defending himself. After all, he was a much better farmer and miner than he was a fighter, yet.

So instead of wasting his time to collect a few measly bones or arrows, he decided to cleverly evade his challengers instead.

"Good bye and good riddance, you skinless freaks," Steve bid them a farewell as he turned his back to them.

Retrieving his trusty stone pickaxe once more, Steve hurried to delve deeper into the mines around him. A few heavy swings had him several blocks

further, and he continued to press on into the world he knew not of. The shaking bones and flying arrows grew quieter as he buried himself deep into the regions of the mountain, and he only hoped that his navigation had not led him astray.

Nearly falling right off of the ledge he had created, the miner finally broke the last block that stood between him and safety. There on the other side was some great subterranean lake—which perhaps had been the one that he had heard when he had fallen in the first place. Steve crawled back a few paces before closing up the tunnel that he had created, leaving every notion of perceived direction behind.

This new chasm was perhaps thrice the size of the first, and Steve wondered how there could possibly be so much beneath the surface he had been obliviously living upon. He could see veins of a myriad of elements, an expansive body of still water, and beyond, the hot fires of settling magma. Lights tumbled into the stony sanctuary from various breaks in the high ceiling and from the distant glow of molten rock, showing the miner his one single exit: a slowly descending tunnel at the far reaches of this seemingly safe sanctum.

"You really deserve this one Steve," he grumbled to himself as he built a block to start his tedious climb back down. "Ever since the day you spawned you've been chasing adventure: staying out late at night and farming zombies, scaling tall ice-caps in the bitter cold, and now, digging straight down and getting yourself lost in a cave. Just what the Wiki warned you about."

CHAPTER 3

Steve paused as he heard the dull groaning of something in the shadows, and had to swallow his fears—and perhaps his lunch—to continue on. The

various rises of scattered blocks made the cave floor hard to maneuver, but it seemed that each second leap was rich with blocks of coal and copper.

Greedily mining the ore, Steve grinned to imagine how many new torches he might craft to light up whatever other hidden treasures resided in this myriad of mineable minerals.

Hoisting his now hefty inventory, Steve trod over the flat cavern floor and approached the great lake, which looked so pure and fresh he almost dove right in. Instead, Steve took out his bucket and filled it up with the valuable liquid. It was uncertain how long he might end up trapped away from his livestock and water well, so he might need to stock up on what he could.

Steve did remember a stream that ran along the side of the mountain, rushing into rapid falls just a ways away from his village. Perhaps this was the other side of it, or the source. Whatever the case, the miner only hoped that he was going in the right direction after all. Saying farewell to his new found atrium of potential wealth, he gathered his pickaxe and headed for the daunting challenge of the magma —and whatever else lay beyond it.

Though he had seen it before, Steve had managed to steer clear of lava that he had encountered on the surface. He had little experience with destructive natural forces, and had only just started mining away from his home and village. The nearer that he came towards the slow spilling substance, the more he was reminded of why he had avoided the hot feature to begin with. It was devilishly red and orange, and the creepy seeping was ominous and hypnotic like a great evil creature slinking about in the dark reaches of the mines.

The textured flow of blocks cut off his route, and he gulped as he measured the thinnest stream of blocks and gambled his jump against it. Upon approaching the threatening liquid, he could almost see the way the fumes of heat danced in sweaty waves mere inches from the useless shank of his pickaxe. Glancing over the obstacle, Steve could see a wide passage that seemed to bring him nearer to his desired destination, and knew that he could not merely seek an easier path.

"It's cool, it's cool. Lava only causes four damage per half second and sets you on fire, it's cool," Steve reminded himself with a shaky voice, taking a few paces back before testing his skills against it.

Holding his breath like he was about to dive right into the magma, Steve raced towards his possible demise and leaped at the last step before the hellish substance. He worriedly slammed his eyes shut as he made the bound, but nearly scared himself silly as he easily reached the other side unhindered. Steve blinked dumbly before looking back at the ridiculously less than challenging task he had cleared, before sheepishly mustering a chuckle.

"Well that was a lot easier than I thought." He smirked to himself and swung his straight leg out to jauntily carry on, when he was halted by a very familiar yet never welcomed sound.

It was a groan—a deep, guttural moan that reverberated along the cave walls in such a tone that it almost sounded like a question or a beg. Steve was statuesque as he stared into the shadowy abyss, and he wasn't sure if his eyes were playing tricks on him, or if he caught sight of some movement down there. Heedless of the knots in his stomach, Steve was too curious not to go down there.

He was no stranger to the creatures that lurked within the mines, in fact, he had encountered zombies more than any other hostile mob be could think of. Yet down in the furthest reaches of a strange chamber, he felt less than confident. For all he knew, there were dozens of them spawning just out of sight. Sliding his stone sword out of his inventory like it was some bottomless bag—which he supposed it was—he raised his arm and new weapon triumphantly. Well, as triumphantly as he could muster while chattering his teeth.

Holding his pixel patch of sword out at the full extension of his arm, Steve sidestepped his way down the block by block descent. Each step seemed like another level of light he lost, and he hung close to the highest part of the ceiling to keep his eye-line clear. Another groan almost made him jump or scream, but instead, he just whirled around in an uncontrollable manner. Swinging at the air as if deterring any potential foe from trying for his life, Steve hustled along the wall in hopes of coming across an exit.

CHAPTER 4

A loud groan from directly beside him summoned a shout from his own throat, and he bashed his sword around until coming into contact with something that flashed red. Noticing his infliction of damage, Steve continued to wildly slice through the air until whatever had been there finally went silent. With

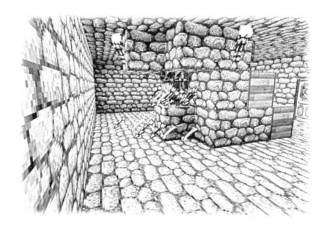

great and erratic huffs, Steve stood above his freshly vanquished foe.

"That's right! Come near me, and, and that'll happen to any one of you! Got it?" he called out to the cave, and heard the trails of his voice echo back. Pretending to have not been frightened in the slightest, he straightened the fixed graphic of his collar.

With the visibility greatly reduced—and getting worse the deeper into the tunnel he trekked—Steve knew that he'd need to give himself the advantage of another torch. The increased visibility and decreased chance of zombies spawning made it too valuable of an asset not to exploit. He was nervous, however, as he reached into his inventory and noticed the shrinking stack of torches he had left. Sure, he was collecting a good lot of coal, but he was short on sticks. Lighting one more torch, Steve turned towards the nearest cavern wall and stuck the thin object against the stone block.

The ceiling was a good deal shorter than Steve had imagined, and it made him feel very closed in and buried. But that did not stop him from adventuring deeper, choosing the leftmost path through the tunnel as it seemed to sport less meandering paths. The various distant groans and moans were haunting, though even with his keen eyes, Steve could not find where they were coming from. That is, until a sudden four block drop at the end of his chosen trail.

Retrieving a torch, Steve left his fear behind on the side of the drop and jumped down, placing the torch directly on the wall behind him. However, he was alarmed by the nearness of another dull groan and the chill of death at the nape of his neck. As he turned, Steve found himself faced with the long-nosed visage of a zombie villager. Initially thinking the creature was an oddly coloured friend, Steve was about to speak when he was struck by the zombie's icy, deceased hands.

"Ahh! Get back!" his attempt to sound intimidating fell on deaf ears, and he clumsily fumbled through his inventory—first selecting his water bucket, then some dirt—before finding his sword once more.

Steve jumped heroically and sliced at his enemy with a violent attack, taking the time as the zombie was stalled to move out of his reach. He flinched though as he was met with the assault of another zombie, who too had found his intrusion of their mine as a hostile act. With defensive swings, Steve fought the two off while stumbling deeper into the mine shaft. As one zombie fell to the swings of his weak sword, another approached him from his right side and moaned a hearty hello.

Wrathful reaching from his foes sent Steve clambering up a few block steps, his sword brandished high as if seeking the glimmer of sunlight that might squeak through spaces in all these millions of blocks. Another few hits had Steve gasping for his final breaths, and he took to the air for a more furious swing of his worn sword. Slamming the weight of his body and fall against the cold stone of his weapon, Steve landed a critical hit upon the square head of his enemy. The third and last of his attackers fell to a flurry of directed blows, and at last, Steve could take a moment to rest.

The bite of some meat he had luckily thought to bring along with him was more satisfying than his conquest, and he eagerly chewed at the slab until it was finished. Upon completion, with his hunger satisfied, Steve could feel the slow return of some of his health. A relieved sigh flew pleasantly out of his mouth, and he carefully counted his torches once more before holding one up to the shadowy walls around him.

"Oh, man." A frown accompanied his realization that he appeared to have reached another dead end. "And here I thought adventure was supposed to be a little more exciting."

CHAPTER 5

The silence was consuming, but his lack of escape was what was truly troubling. He glanced around once more, holding his flaming item up to the walls as though he might be able to see through them. He was about to give up and turn tail, when something on a block caught his attention. Approaching it carefully, Steve narrowed his eyes towards the very small trace of some black smoke. Curiously tilting his head, he wondered what it might mean.

"What the..." he began to ask, but was stalled by some loud hissing that came from right behind him. His eyes widened as he recognized the sound, and immediately jumped away from the source. "A creeper?!"

A huge explosion knocked him for a loop, but he managed to hold onto some remnants of his health as he fell through the now destroyed floor into some built stronghold. Blocks fell around him as he noticed a few player-placed torches fell off the walls that had just caved in. He realized that it must have been the smoke from torches that had been visible through the thin blocks. The newly found light was comforting, but the large space of player-made structure concerned him. Steve had never run into another player, and he had hoped to have been more prepared for when he did. After all, his shack by the village was still just made simply of wood.

The structured shaft was beautiful. It was perfectly symmetrical, well lit, had decorative pillars and several door lining the walls. Although at first Steve wondered what the room might have been for, he soon came to discover by peeking through the doors that there were several mining veins, most of which had already been tapped. Most, save for one particular collection.

Pushing the door open, Steve's eyes glittered as they snagged on the many pale-blue speckled stones. Though he had never seen it before, he could clearly identify these as diamond-laced blocks. If he could only get his hands on some of it, his armor and weapons could be crafted like the best.

However, Steve glanced down at the weak stone sword in his hand, and knew the same poor craftsmanship was present in his pickaxe. Such a valuable and strong ore as diamond, he knew he could not mine.

His skills and tools were far too weak to permit his greedy desires. Looking up hopefully at the blocks, Steve committed himself to at least trying but once.

Raising his stone pickaxe as though it was the key to the great doors of heaven, Steve aimed his swing at the white and blue riddled blocks. One step stood between him and perhaps plundering this stronghold, and bravely, he took it. Yet his stone pickaxe would never even get to make contact with the elusive block, as the very ground beneath him dropped.

"Ahh!" Steve shouted as he fell through the deceptive floor, drowning out the sound of a Redstone contraption giving way.

The fall was great, and as he cleared the narrow shaft right below the room of diamond blocks, Steve met the fate intended for any who might steal from that strange miner. A great lake of magma roared beneath him, and a vast chasm of otherwise darkness enveloped him. Hurriedly shifting through the air, Steve managed to hug the nearest wall, and catching brief sight of something hanging along it, reached out. Great hangs of vines hissed against him as he fell against it, and hidden inside its magnificent growth, a ladder expertly stopped his fall.

Dangling over certain death, Steve struggled to keep the life inside of himself. As his heart dropped back out of his throat and into his chest, he released a long held breath and held dearer onto the ladder that had saved him. It was clear that whoever had designed such a trap wasn't daring enough to leave himself without a means of salvation if he or she had ever fallen through it, and such a foresight had saved Steve from his own fate.

He eagerly climbed back up the ladder as if it was burning beneath him—as he had never been too fond of heights, nor swinging just above a massive body of magma, he then discovered. There was a ledge just a ways up the wall, which remained a good drop below the bottom of the stronghold from the looks of it. Steve pulled himself up at last, not bothering to turn back and gaze once more into the talons of demise.

The ledge was very flat and hard, and though the wall had sported runs of ivy, it appeared that nothing more grew on the barren top of this stage. It was lit —surprisingly—by more than just the luminescence of the lava that laid below. In fact, several torches lit up a narrow passage at the far side, though it was becoming difficult to trust anything in that mine.

CHAPTER 6

Approaching the torch-lit trail, Steve paused before taking a step off the seemingly secure ledge. It seemed just far too easy, to simply walk away from something such as that trap. And surely it was, for though Steve armed himself with his stone sword, no weapon would help him navigate the labyrinth of shafts before him. They were clearly made by a player, as each one seemed far too straight to have been naturally occurring.

"This place is a maze! Is there even an exit, at all?" Steve asked nobody, or perhaps anyone who might have been listening: the stone, the pickaxe, the vines which still drooped down around him.

Pushing past one wall of vines, Steve swatted at a second as if he was angry with them. His frustration was clearly more with himself than anything: himself, for wandering so carelessly and digging until he fell through the very ground; himself, for delving deeper into the caves in search of some adventure; himself, for being tricked by some obvious trap and nearly burning to death. Still though, he swatted at the ivy until something just beyond it caught his attention.

It was tall, whatever it was, and emerged from the darkness like some apparition. What seemed like downy, violet snowflakes fell around it in such serenity that it seemed to be some sentient sage. Though its elongated, rectangular features stretched longer than Steve could possibly stand, it was gentle with the small, grassy block it carried. Staring through the vines, Steve was stunned to watch the creature disappear entirely for a spell. Again though, it returned, further down the reaches of one particular tunnel.

"Wait, come back!" his faltering voice was swept up in the endless vastness of the mines.

As the giant teleported once more, Steve found himself entranced and enchanted, galvanized to explore further through the shaft. Carried away by his curiosity, Steve plunged into the middle tunnel despite the very poor lighting. Every turn, a torch would illuminate his steps for far too short a time to have permitted a sense of security, but regardless, he trudged on. The quick flashes of his tempting taunter appeared beyond his visibility every time, and though he made chase, it seemed that he only fell further and further behind.

Steve paused to catch his breath, though it too was summoned to seek that evasive being he knew so little of. Leaning on the wall, he took a second to scan his surroundings in what little light he had. The usually light grey blocks had become darker before he had taken notice, and he gently touched the soft and moist surface of the flat object.

"Dirt?" Steve identified it, knowing the substance

very well. It must have been blocks of soil—the same kind that the mysterious creature had been towing along. "I must be getting close to the surface!"

Racing down the narrow shaft, Steve flung himself towards the possibility of some end. His pickaxe swung over his shoulder like the two were dancing with joy, the handle so firmly clasped in his blistered and callused palms. The farther he travelled down that marked path, the more he was certain that he was getting close. He could hear the running of water, the familiar sounds of farm animals, even wind in some trees.

CHAPTER 7

At last, down one abrupt corner, a gentle fall of moonlight tugged at him to pursue. He had forgotten just how long he had been lost inside the caves, but it was clear that night had fallen in his absence. Steve sprinted towards his exit, dragging his nearly full inventory behind his bobbing back. As he breached the surface, he was greeted with the vastness of the star-pixeled sky and the soft caress of the brilliant moon. The clear air felt so fresh and chilled, he bathed in it like a clear oasis pool.

His eyes traced the familiar arrangement of stars and the arc of the lunar cycle, and wagered that it had been night for quite some time now. Steve turned back to look up at where he had emerged from, and was surprised to find how far away from the mountain that he had come. In fact, he had somehow managed to work all the way through it and onto the other side entirely. Despite the joy he felt from finally finding his way out of the mines, he was disappointed with just how far left he had to go. Granted, it would take far less time to travel on the surface that it had taken him to accidentally stumble through the tunnels—so long as he made certain not to fall through any more breaks in the ground.

There was no good in waiting for the sun to rise before he would start on his journey back, as he was still uncertain how near to that stranger's stronghold he remained. But before he would start on his way back, he took another last look around. There, striding slowly in the distance, was that strange purplish creature that had led him out of the maze beneath the surface. He smiled as he watched the creature pause and look back at him, and the two met gazes for a few long seconds.

"Thank you, strange Enderman." Steve firmly offered his thanks to the large thing, and though they stared at one another for a good while longer, it appeared that the Enderman did not appreciate his gratitude at all.

As Steve blinked, his savior disappeared once more. At first he took it as a sign of understanding, and was about to leave, when something flashed behind him. Steve gasped as he took some damage, jumping away from the source in agony and shock. As he furiously looked around, he caught only the fragmented few purple flakes that settled as the Enderman teleported away from him. Again, another hit was inflicted, and Steve grew increasingly terrified and worried. He would not wait for a third hit, and hurriedly ran off in the direction he certainly hoped would lead him home, glancing over his shoulder at every opportunity.

The steep drop of a hill almost stalled him, but another violent attack sent him over the edge and tumbling towards a still lake. Steve held his breath as the water maternally caught him, embracing him in all of his fear and folly. As the Enderman appeared behind him once more, he was pleasantly surprised to witness the creature taking harm from the water. Steve tried his best to swing his weapon while swimming, but it seemed as though his attacks were unnecessary. Popping in and out of sight, the Enderman called out as it sustained more pain. At last, the water became still and silent, save for Steve's frantic paddling and breathing.

The water was deep and dark, but it was something like a warm bed after all that he had encountered. He gently waded over to the shore, and coughed a few times as he pulled himself out of the water and dripped some tracks across the sand bank. Wringing out his matching blue clothes and his inventory sack, he shook his head and decided to stomach some of the now moist bread he had been carrying along with him.

CHAPTER 8

As he chewed on the soggy loaf, Steve strode towards his village. The mountain that he had to pass was steep and now appeared quite cruel, despite the plump puffs of wool that bounced atop it in the form of sheep. He glowered as he finished the last bit of crust, and returned a more menacing tool to his hand than a loaf of bread. His sword provided him with some semblance of courage, and it led him back to his home.

Perhaps the orange horizon should have alerted or warned him, but he paid it no heed. After all, the sky always appeared to be that amber sap-like hue just seconds before the sun would rise. As as that great square sun bounded over the mountain-clad landscape, Steve was filled with a sense of accomplishment and pride. Here he was, a novice young miner who, by every fault of his own, got himself lost in a maze of caves and shafts, and by every merit of his own, succeeded in finding his way home. Yes, he truly displayed everything that an aspiring adventurer might sport.

The beautiful sun was so majestic to him: the sole bright and luminous pixel seemed mined and placed so perfectly is was as though the heavens had a pickaxe of star matter. Yet the farther into the great cloud-blotched sky it rose, the more curious it became that the glowing of his now visible village was not due to the change in colour with a sunrise.

Steve rushed to peer over the gently sloping hills of farmlands and pastures, and was heartbroken as he found all the huts in the village brightly ablaze. There were great craters around the town, presumably from exploding creepers or barrages of TNT. And finally, he could see the distant remains of what was once his wooden lodging.

Falling to his trembling knees, Steve gaped at the destruction that had griefed his entire village. His sword, something that had seemed so powerful and valiant as to have saved him before, felt worthless and limp in his hand. His hefty bag of bounty and new found treasures, which he had been so proud of and excited to craft with, seemed like dead weight on his slumping shoulders.

"It's so much easier to destroy, than to build," he lamented the fallen village softly. Lifting his inventory and himself back to his feet, he stared out at the hungry flames. "I'll find you, other miner. And when I do, you'll regret this."

Steve turned his back to the ashes of a place he once sought, a place he once called his home, and he left it. What stood before him was a much greater challenge than it had been to farm some livestock, to haul lumber, or to build his humble shack. What stood before him, in the form of a massive mountain that harbored some of his greatest challenges, was the adventure that he had sought, and the means by which to seek his vengeance. Or perhaps, just another hole to fall down.

MAP

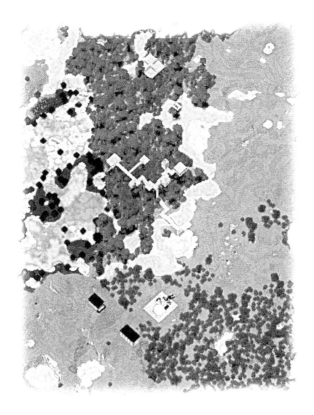

GET INVOLVED

If you've enjoyed the story, please take a little time to leave an Amazon review. This helps enormously

Please leave constructive comment in your review on how this book could be improved or even plot ideas, that can be used in future Wimpy Fan books. You will receive FULL credit in print!

ABOUT THE AUTHOR

Wimpy Fan has been writing Minecraft, Wimpy Diary and Adventure Time fan fiction for the last 3 and a half years.

He is the author of over a dozen Minecraft short stories including the 'Amazing Adventures of Minecraft Steve' series, and has published articles on numerous 'Fan Fiction' blog sites.

wimpy.fan@yahoo.com